A GOLDEN BOOK · NEW YORK

Just a Little Critter Collection book, characters, text, and images © 2005 Mercer Mayer.
LITTLE CRITTER, MERCER MAYER'S LITTLE CRITTER, and MERCER MAYER'S LITTLE CRITTER and Logo are
registered trademarks of Orchard House Licensing Company. All rights reserved under International
and Pan-American Copyright Conventions. Published in the United States by Golden Books, an
imprint of Random House Children's Books, a division of Random House, Inc., New York, and
simultaneously in Canada by Random House of Canada Limited, Toronto. Golden Books, A Golden
Book, and the G colophon are registered trademarks of Random House, Inc. The material contained
in this book was taken from the following Golden Books publications: *Just for You,* © 1975 Mercer
Mayer; *When I Get Bigger,* © 1983 Mercer Mayer; *I Was So Mad,* © 1983 Mercer Mayer;
All By Myself, © 1983 Mercer Mayer*; Just Go to Bed,* © 1983 Mercer Mayer; *Just a Mess,*
© 1987 Mercer Mayer; and *I Just Forgot,* © 1988 Mercer Mayer.
ISBN: 0-375-83255-6
www.goldenbooks.com
MANUFACTURED IN CHINA
10 9 8 7 6 5 4 3

JUST A LITTLE CRITTER® COLLECTION

Written and illustrated by Mercer Mayer

CONTENTS

This morning I wanted to make breakfast just for you . . . but the eggs were too slippery.

I wanted to wash the floor
just for you,
but the soap was too bubbly.

I wanted to put away the dishes
just for you,
but the floor was too wet.

I wanted to carry the groceries
just for you,
but the bag broke.

I ate my sandwich
just for you,
but not my crusts.

I wanted to take a nap
just for you,
but the bed was too bouncy.

I wanted to mow the lawn
just for you,
but I was too little.

I picked an apple
just for you,
but on the way home
I got hungry.

I wanted to set the table
just for you,
but the TV was too loud.

I wanted to
not splash in my bath
just for you . . .

. . . but there was a storm.

I wanted to do something very special,

just for you.

And I did it.

When I get bigger I'll be able to do lots of things.

I'll go to the corner store by myself . . .

. . . and spend my allowance
on anything I want.

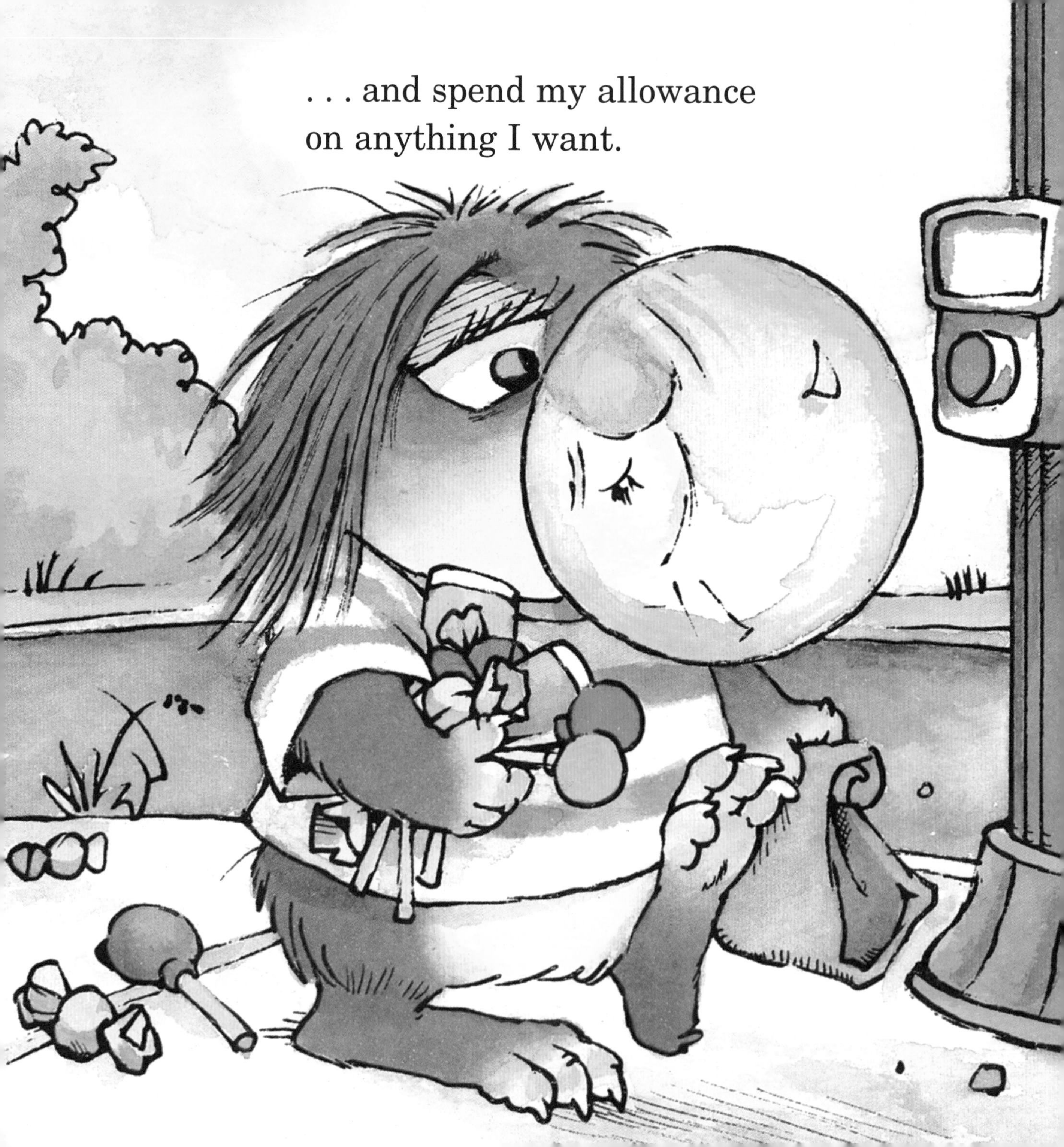

I'll wait until the light is green.
Then I'll look both ways for cars
before I cross the street.

I'll have my own watch
and I'll tell everyone
what time it is.

I'll go on a bus
to Grandma and
Grandpa's.

When I get bigger I'll have a real leather football . . .

. . . my own radio, and a pair of super-pro roller skates.

I'll have a two-wheeler and a paper route.
I'll make lots of money.

At the playground I'll
help the little kids
on the swings.

I'll pick out
my own boots at
the shoe store.

I'll make a phone call
and dial it myself.

I'll order something from a catalog . . .

. . . and it will come in the mail.

When I get bigger I'll camp out
in the backyard all night long.

Or I'll stay up to
see the end of the
late movie.
Even if I get sleepy,
I won't go to bed.

But right now I have to go to bed . . .

. . . because Mom and Dad say . . .

. . . I'm not bigger yet.

I WAS SO MAD

BY
MERCER MAYER

I wanted to keep some frogs in the bathtub but Mom wouldn't let me.

I was so mad.

I wanted to play
with my little sister's
dollhouse but Dad
wouldn't let me.

I was so mad.

I wanted to play
hide-and-seek in
the clean sheets
but Grandma said,
"No, you can't."

I was just so mad.

I wanted to water the garden
but Grandpa said,
"No, you can't."

So I decided to decorate the house but Grandpa said, "No, you can't do that, either."

Was I ever mad.

Dad said, "Why don't you play in the sandbox?"

I didn't want to do that.

Mom said, "Why don't you
play on the slide?"

I didn't want to do that, either.
I was too mad.

I wanted to practice my juggling show, instead.

But Mom said, "No, you can't."

I wanted to tickle the goldfish but Mom said, "Leave the goldfish alone."

"You won't let me do anything I want to do," I said. "I guess I'll run away."

That's how mad I was.

So I packed my wagon
with my favorite toys.

And I packed a bag of cookies to eat on the way.

Then I walked out the front door.
But my friends were going to the
park to play ball.
"Can you come, too?" they asked.

And Mom said I could.

I'll run away tomorrow if I'm still so mad.

I can get out of bed all by myself.

I can button
my overalls.

I can brush my fur.

I can put on my socks . . .

and tie my shoes.

I can pour some juice
for my little sister . . .

and help her eat breakfast.

I can pull a duck for her.

I can drive my truck.

I can ride my bike.

I can give a drink
to my bear.

I can kick my ball . . .

and roll on the ground.

I can pound with
my hammer.

I can sail my boat.

I can look after
my little sister.

I can help Dad trim a bush . . .

or ice a cake for Mom.

I can look at a
book and find
a mouse.

I can color a picture.

I can put my toys away . . .

and get into my pajamas.

I can brush my teeth.

I can put myself to bed . . .

but I can't go to sleep
without a story.

Good night.

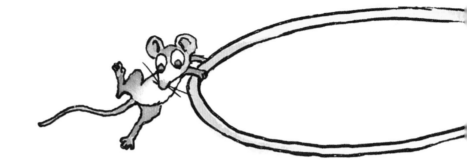

I'm a cowboy and
I round up cows.
I can lasso anything.

Dad says . . .

"It's time for the cowboy
to come inside and get
ready for bed."

I'm a general and I have
to stop the enemy army
with my tank.

Dad says . . .

"It's time for the general to take a bath."

I'm a space cadet and I zoom
to the moon.

I capture a robot
with my ray gun.

Dad says . . .

"This giant robot has captured the space cadet and is going to put him in the bathtub right now."

Dad says, "It's time for the sea monster to have a snack."

I'm a zookeeper feeding
my hungry animals.

Dad says . . .

"Feeding time is over. Here are
the zookeeper's pajamas."

Dad says,
"The bandit chief
has caught you
so put on
your pajamas."

But I'm a race car driver
and I just speed away.

Dad says, "The race is over.
Now put on these pajamas
and go to bed."

I'm a bunny hopping
around my garden.

Dad says . . .

"But I'm a bunny and bunnies don't sleep in a bed."

Mom says, "Shhh!"
Dad says, "Go to sleep."

Well, maybe a tired bunny
could sleep in a bed . . .

just this once.

JUST A MESS

BY
MERCER MAYER

Today I couldn't find my baseball mitt.

I looked in my tree house.

I looked under the back steps.

I asked Mom if she had seen it.
She said I should try my room.

I never thought to look there.
What a mess!

Mom said it was time
to clean my room.
So I asked her to help.

She said, "You made the mess,
so you can clean up the mess."

Dad was working in the yard.
He said he was too busy to help me.

My little sister said, "No way!"
And the baby didn't understand.

I just did it myself.

First, I put a few things in the closet.

I put my clothes
in the drawers.

I straightened up
my games.

I shut the lid
to my toy box

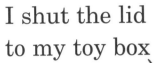

and put away my books.

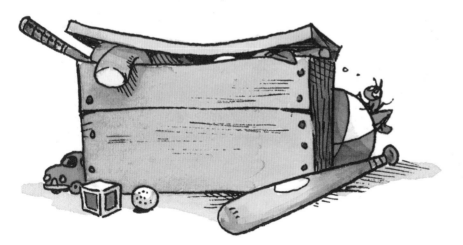

The rest of the mess could fit under my bed,
so I put it there.

Then I made the bed.
Won't Mom be pleased.

I thought I might wash the floor.

But Mom said, "NO!"
So I just vacuumed instead.

Everything was just about perfect.

Then I noticed that my pillow was missing.

I looked on the other side of my bed,

and guess what I found?

My baseball mitt.

Sometimes I remember,
and sometimes I just forget.

This morning I remembered to brush my teeth, but I forgot to make my bed.

I put my dishes in the sink after breakfast,
but I forgot to put the milk away.

I almost forgot to feed the puppy, but he reminded me.

Grrrr

I didn't forget to water the plants. They looked fine to me.

I didn't forget to feed the goldfish.
He just didn't look hungry. I'll
do it now, Mom.

I got ready for school.
I even got to the school bus on time.

But I forgot my lunch box.

Mom brought it to school for me.
Thanks, Mom.

After school, I went outside to play in the rain.
I remembered to put on my rain slicker.

But I forgot my rubber boots.

When I came inside for a snack, I didn't forget to take my boots off. I left them on because I was going right back outside.

I had cookies and milk.

I was just going to eat three cookies, but
I forgot to count them.

I didn't forget to shut the refrigerator door, though.
I just wasn't finished eating yet.

When Dad came home from work, I was supposed to get his paper. I didn't forget—the puppy got it first.

I know it's time for bed. I didn't forget.

Of course I'll remember to pick up my toys when
I'm finished playing with them.

I took my bath and remembered to wash behind my ears.

I didn't use soap, but I didn't forget to. I just don't like soap.

I guess I did forget to pick up my toys.

But there is one thing I never forget.

I always remember to have Mom
read me a bedtime story. And I always remember
to kiss her good night.